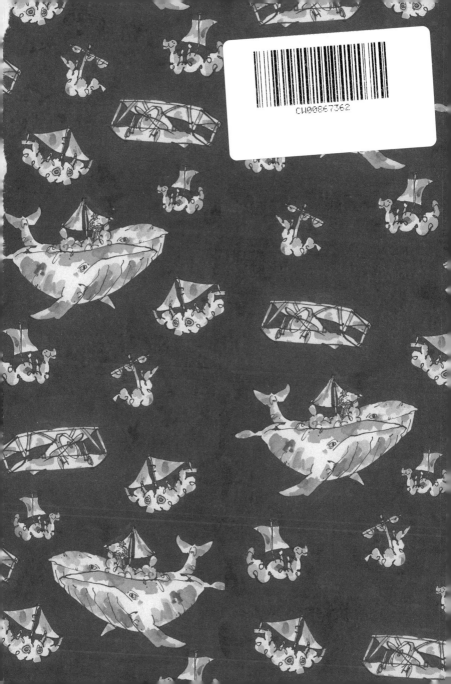

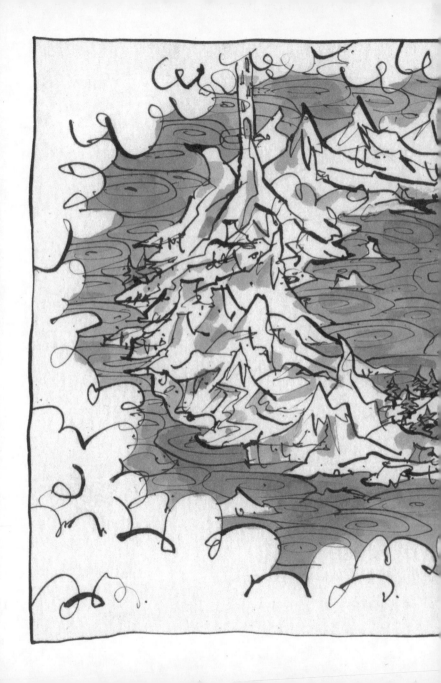

Uncle Pete

and the

Boy Who Couldn't Sleep

David C. Flanagan

Illustrated by Will Hughes

LITTLE DOOR BOOKS

Dedicated to my son, David, for all our past adventures, and those yet to come.

David C. Flanagan

Thanks to Dave and Will for coming on this new adventure with us. Extra special thanks to our young reviewers Isaac and Caiden.

Little Door Books

First published in 2021 in Great Britain
by Little Door Books

www.littledoorbooks.co.uk

Text © 2021 David C. Flanagan

Illustrations © Will Hughes

A CIP catalogue record for this book is available from the British Library upon request

ISBN: 978-1-9162054-3-7

Design and layout by Augusta Kirkwood

Printed in Poland by Totem

Contents

Chapter 1   1

Chapter 2   11

Chapter 3   23

Chapter 4   41

Chapter 5   55

Chapter 6   75

Chapter 7   89

Chapter 8   103

Chapter 1

Harry never went to sleep. Not ever. In fact, Harry had been wide-awake since the day he was born.

It didn't matter what his mum and dad tried. And they had tried absolutely everything to get Harry to go to sleep. All of the things that normally helped children get to sleep just didn't work with Harry.

Mum and Dad had read him stories - lots and lots of stories. So many stories, in fact, that all the bookshops in town had run out of books. Even the library didn't have any stories left which Harry hadn't heard.

Famous writers heard about Harry and tried to create new stories they were sure would work and put him to sleep. Some of the stories were so good they were made into films and the writers got even more famous and rich. But none of their amazing tales ever helped Harry get to sleep.

Someone told Harry's mum and dad that warm milky drinks helped people get to sleep. So, they tried giving him warm

milky drinks. And then cold milky drinks.
Mum and Dad even borrowed a whole
herd of cows from a friendly farmer and
put them in the garden to make sure they
always had milky drinks for Harry. But
still Harry stayed awake (though all the
milk made him want to pee a lot more).

Mum and Dad sang him lullabies until their throats got sore. When they'd run out of lullabies to sing, they tried singing songs they'd liked when they were growing up – even though they were mostly rubbish – but still nothing worked.

All of Harry's aunts, uncles and cousins took turns at coming round to his house at night, singing him songs. And when that didn't work, everyone in the town had a go too, singing outside Harry's house every evening until they all got fed up and went home.

World famous rock stars heard about Harry not sleeping and organised a special quiet concert in the local park to try and put him to sleep. They even wrote a song called Please Go to Sleep, Harry, We're All So Tired, and did a video too. But it didn't work.

Although Harry loved all the stories and songs, and the milky drinks, he never, ever felt sleepy.

It wasn't Harry's fault. It was just the way he'd been born. He had never known what it was like to sleep, so he didn't miss it.

Harry's friends at school were the only ones not bothered by him being awake all the time, though they were always saying that sleeping was brilliant as it gave your body a good rest after playing and learning all day. And, at the weekend, you could sleep until lunchtime and then watch cartoons.

His friends also told him all about dreams and how they were like amazing pictures and stories in your head, but they only happened when you were sleeping. They even told Harry how, sometimes (usually after eating too much cheese before bedtime or watching a scary programme on TV) you got nightmares – dreams that weren't fun at all. But, none of it was real and everything was ok when you woke up.

Although Harry didn't feel tired at all, he thought it might be nice to be able to sleep and enjoy a good dream. Even a nightmare sounded pretty interesting. He ate loads of cheese at night to see if that might work, but it didn't.

Of course, Mum and Dad had taken Harry to see the doctor because they were worried he might have something wrong with him that made him stay awake all the time. They'd first gone when Harry was a baby as he didn't sleep at all.

The doctor had checked Harry all

over and said he was fine. As Harry got older, Mum and Dad kept going back to the doctor as he still wasn't sleeping. The doctor examined him and, every time, said he was the fittest and healthiest boy he'd ever seen. When Harry was a bit older again, the puzzled doctor said he'd get some other doctors to look at Harry too, just to make sure there was nothing wrong.

And so, all of the doctors from Harry's town had come to see him, followed by all of the doctors from other towns. Soon, doctors from far away countries came to look at Harry, but none of them could find a single thing wrong with him. He just couldn't sleep, that was all.

As Harry got older, he started to get more and more bored being awake all the time, so his family carried on taking turns staying up with him all night. Sometimes, Mum would go to bed and Dad would sit beside Harry, trying to make up new stories or sing songs he hadn't heard. The next night it would be Mum's turn to stay up with Harry while Dad had a sleep.

And that was how they had done things for years and years and years.

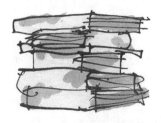

Chapter 2

Harry's mum and dad were pretty tired. In fact, his whole family and most of the town were absolutely exhausted. They all loved Harry very much, but just wished that he'd get some sleep.

Then, one day, when Mum and Dad had just about given up trying to find new ways of getting Harry to sleep, there was a knock at the front door of their house.

When Dad opened it, he saw a tall man with a mop of black, curly hair on his head and a big black beard standing on the doorstep. The man was dressed in dusty, ragged clothes and was carrying a huge rucksack on his back.

Then Dad recognized the man. It was Uncle Pete.

Uncle Pete was Dad's brother. He was an explorer. He'd been off exploring mountains, jungles and deserts for years and years, since before Harry was born. In fact, Uncle Pete had been away for so long that everyone in the family had pretty much forgotten about him. He'd never sent a postcard for ages, so they thought he must have been eaten by a lion or a shark. Or maybe he was just lost.

Uncle Pete said he had come home from exploring to get some new underpants and buy a supply of beans – Uncle Pete absolutely loved beans on toast, but he couldn't always have them when he was exploring. Most of the places he visited didn't have shops that sold beans in tomato sauce.

While Uncle Pete was in town, buying his beans and fresh underpants – it was Uncle Pete's rule always to wear clean underpants, just in case he ended up in hospital on an adventure – he noticed how tired everyone that he met was.

The man in the underpants shop was fast asleep with his head on the counter, so Uncle Pete left the money for his new pants beside him, with a note saying: "I've just bought 20 pairs of pants. Here's the money. Best wishes, Uncle Pete."

Everyone in the supermarket looked exhausted too. Uncle Pete thought there must have been a huge party in the town for something and maybe they'd all just stayed up too late.

Then he suddenly remembered he had a nephew called Harry whom he'd never met. He'd decided to come and visit Harry and his family before going away on another expedition.

When Uncle Pete came into Harry's house, he saw how tired Mum and Dad looked, just like all the other townspeople. Harry, meanwhile, looked bright and full of energy. He was excited to meet his explorer uncle for the first time.

"Pleased to meet you Harry," said Uncle Pete. "You're the only person I've met today that doesn't look tired."

"That's because I'm not tired," said Harry, who was sorting out his things for school the next day. "I'm never tired."

"Everybody gets tired," laughed Uncle Pete. "Even me, and I'm an explorer.

There was this one time when I was being chased by a furious polar bear after it lost a snowball fight with me. It chased me for days and I was so tired I eventually had to stop and give it my scarf and a cinema ticket. It went off quite happy after that."

"But I've never, ever been tired," said Harry. "I've never been to sleep, and I've never had a dream."

Uncle Pete didn't believe Harry at first. He was just about to start telling him another explorer story, about the time he was being chased by a furious tiger in the jungle – after trying to take a selfie with it – and was so tired he had to stop and give the tiger his phone, just so he could get some sleep, when Harry's Mum and Dad said it was true he'd never slept.

They told Uncle Pete the whole story,

listing all of the different things they had tried to get Harry to sleep, and how none of them had worked.

"Hmmm," said Uncle Pete, taking off his floppy hat and scratching his dusty hair (which looked as if it hadn't been washed for a very long time). "I might just be able to help you, Harry."

Uncle Pete opened up his big rucksack and tipped it upside down. All of his explorer stuff poured out onto the carpet, but Harry's mum and dad were so tired, they didn't care.

In amongst all of Uncle Pete's pots and pans, ropes, flags, binoculars, sandwiches, muddy clothes, tins of beans and new underpants, was an old, tattered map.

"Here it is! I knew I still had this map,"
he said, spreading it on the floor.

The map was of a country Mum and
Dad had never seen before. It was shaped
like a crescent moon and looked as if it
was covered in high mountains.

"What's this place called?" yawned
Dad.

"It doesn't have a name," said Uncle Pete. "I discovered it by accident when I was exploring years ago. I even drew the map myself. It's a strange place because it always seems to be nighttime there. If I can find it again, there's someone there that might just be able to help Harry get to sleep."

"Who?" asked Mum and Dad.

"No time to waste!" said Uncle Pete as he stuffed all his things back in his rucksack. "If young Harry's going to get to sleep, I need to find that place again, right now!"

And with that, he pulled on his rucksack, and ran out of the door.

Dad ran to the door and shouted after him: "But where are you going?"

Chapter 2

"No time to explain!" shouted Uncle Pete as he ran down the road, leaving a trail of pots and pans and bits of explorer stuff clattering behind him.

Chapter 3

Uncle Pete ran all the way back to his explorer's house, which was in a forest by a lake, a few miles away from where Harry and his parents lived.

Uncle Pete had built the house himself using old trees that had fallen down in stormy weather. He'd left some of the branches on so squirrels and birds could live on the walls of his house as Uncle Pete loved animals.

On the roof of his house was a garden where Uncle Pete grew potatoes and strawberries because he liked chips and homemade strawberry jam almost as much as he liked beans on toast.

Uncle Pete's house was very untidy but that was the way he liked it. Inside he had lots of books about exploring, and hundreds of copies of the cookbook he had written himself about how to make the perfect beans on toast, chips and strawberry jam.

On the walls there were photographs of all the amazing places Uncle Pete had visited as an explorer, along with a certificate he'd been awarded for growing a world record breaking strawberry that was as big as a football.

Dashing inside the house, Uncle Pete quickly made some strawberry jam sandwiches and put them into his rucksack along with 23 tins of beans and six loaves of bread.

He then got out his old map of the strange, moon-shaped country, spread it on his table and scratched his head. "Hmm, let me see," he said out loud to himself. "What would be the quickest way to find this place again I wonder? Yes, I know!"

Uncle Pete ran out into his garden to look for his shed. His grass hadn't been cut for years and the garden was like a jungle, so Uncle Pete couldn't find the shed at first. He thrashed around for 20 minutes before he spotted the shed roof, just peeking out above the very long grass and bushes.

Uncle Pete's shed wasn't like a normal one at all though. It was absolutely huge and entirely made of old bean tins, which Uncle Pete had collected over the years. Once he'd gathered enough tins, he'd flattened them out with a hammer and nailed them all together to make the walls, roof and doors of the shed.

At first the shed had been bright and shiny, though it smelled strongly of tomato sauce – Uncle Pete hadn't always remembered to rinse the tins when he'd finished the beans. Now it was all just starting to look a bit rusty.

He pulled open the shed's big tin doors, which were stiff and creaky. Inside it was very dark, but Uncle Pete always carried an explorer torch in one of the pockets of his trousers, beside the packet of chewy honey cough sweets he used to make friends with honey badgers (furious little creatures who start fights with dangerous snakes and hate absolutely everyone, except Uncle Pete).

Inside was a rickety old red aeroplane. It had two wings, one on top and one down below – it was called a biplane – and a big wooden propeller on its nose. There was no roof over the pilot's seat – it was just open to the wind and rain, but Uncle Pete always wore special flying goggles.

The plane was so old that it was covered in cobwebs, dust and rust. There were holes in the wings and one of the wheels was missing – Uncle Pete couldn't remember where it had gone, but thought he might have hit the top of a tree or a building the last time he'd been flying, knocking off the wheel.

Uncle Pete stood on a wooden box and peered inside the plane.

A tiny brown mouse had made her home in the pilot's seat. The mouse stared back at him, annoyed at being disturbed.

"I'm terribly sorry," said Uncle Pete to the mouse. "I'm needing to use my plane and wonder if I could ask you to move? I have an old seat in a warm corner of my shed that you're welcome to use."

Everyone knows that mice like good manners and so, because Uncle Pete had asked politely, the mouse nodded sadly and gathered up her stuff (mostly bits of cheese). Uncle Pete was surprised to see that the mouse had a little suitcase.

He was more surprised when the mouse spoke to him. He'd seen many unusual things as an explorer, but never a talking mouse. A mouse with a suitcase was even more unusual.

"Where are you going?" it asked him,

as it packed its cheese into a suitcase marked with the letters 'TM'.

"Um, on an adventure," replied Uncle Pete.

"Do you need any help?" asked the mouse, who then introduced herself as 'TM'.

"It stands for Tiny Mouse," she explained. "Because I'm tiny – I was the smallest in my family – and I'm also a mouse."

"I can see that," replied Uncle Pete. "Can you read a map?"

"Of course I can read a map," replied TM, rolling her eyes. "I'm a mouse. I can do anything. Will there be cheese involved in this adventure?"

"Well, there are beans and strawberry jam, and, yes, quite possibly cheese too," said Uncle Pete. "You're welcome to come along, if it's ok with your family."

"I don't have a family anymore," said TM sadly. "They all got eaten by a cat a few years ago. I only just escaped and ran into your shed to hide. I've been living here for years, inside your plane. I know how it all works too."

"Great! said Uncle Pete. "You can read the map and help with the flying! No time to waste though, we have to get going."

"Where?" asked TM.

"Give me a hand getting the plane ready and then I'll explain on the way."

♦

Uncle Pete rummaged around in the piles of rusty junk surrounding the plane and found an old pram wheel. He tied the wheel onto the bottom of the plane to replace its missing one. Finally, he got some old newspapers and TM helped him glue them over all the holes in the wings.

"As good as new!" said Uncle Pete, throwing his rucksack into the back of the plane and pulling on his flying goggles. "Let's get this thing into the air and begin our adventure!"

"I don't have goggles!" said TM, suddenly worried she'd have to stay behind. Uncle Pete rummaged around in his rucksack and found a pair of old sunglasses. He fastened a thick rubber band to the legs and handed them to TM.

"Use these," he said. "They're a bit big, but they'll do the job."

Uncle Pete unfolded the old map of the strange looking land they were heading for and taped it onto the controls of his aeroplane. TM ran up onto his shoulder so she could get a good look at the map.

"That's where we're heading?" she asked. "Is it north, south, east or west from here?"

"I don't know," said Uncle Pete. "I found it by accident and can't remember how to get back there. And it only appears when it's dark. We'll have to fly around a bit and see if I spot anything familiar."

TM didn't think this sounded like a sensible way to find anything, but said: "Ok, let's go!"

Uncle Pete turned the starter key on his plane, but nothing happened. There was no noise from the engine and the propeller didn't move.

"Fuel!" he shouted. "We have no fuel!"

Uncle Pete then remembered how, on his last adventure in the plane, he'd run out of fuel just before he'd made it back home safely. The engine had stopped, and he'd had to glide back into the garden, knocking off the wheel in the process.

He jumped out of the seat and rummaged around in his shed, looking for a fuel container. They were all empty.

Uncle Pete then spotted an old jam jar full of silvery dust up on a shelf at the back of the shed. He unscrewed the top and poured the mysterious powder into the plane's fuel tank

"What's that stuff?" asked TM.

"I believe it's stardust," said Uncle Pete.

"I got it a long time ago from the person we need to visit in the place we're trying to find again. It's very useful stuff, I'm told, though I'm not sure it works in engines."

"Stardust? That's not a real thing, is it?" asked TM, not really believing Uncle Pete. "Stardust is just in stories."

"You're a talking mouse and I grow giant strawberries," said Uncle Pete. "Anything is possible. Are you ready?"

"That's true" replied TM. "Well, let's see if it works!"

Uncle Pete jumped back into the pilot's seat and turned the key.

The plane engine made a loud bang and spluttered into life in a huge cloud of sparkly smoke. Uncle Pete steered it out of the shed, pushed the throttle – which was like an accelerator on a car – and roared off down the garden, the propeller cutting all the long grass as they went.

Just when TM thought they were going to crash into the trees at the end of the garden, Uncle Pete pulled back on the controls and the old plane took off into the night sky, a trail of stardust twinkling behind it. They were on their way.

Chapter 4

Even Uncle Pete was amazed at how well the plane worked with a fuel tank full of stardust. They climbed higher and higher into the night sky. It was freezing, so TM scrambled into the chest pocket of Uncle Pete's explorer jacket to stay warm, her nose poking out the top so she could read the old map.

They flew north all night, and then east most of the following day. The day after that, they flew south for a few hours, and then west for a bit, before turning east and then north again.

Uncle Pete tied some string onto the controls of the plane so TM could fly the plane from his chest pocket when he was sleeping – she was a good pilot. When TM slept, Uncle Pete flew. When they were both awake, they took turns at flying, reading the map and sharing out the food.

They passed over countless amazing lands – deserts, mountains, glaciers, rivers, jungles, cities and tiny villages – but there was no sign of them getting any

closer to the special place on Uncle Pete's
map.

"Perhaps we'd get a better view if we
went higher!" shouted TM over the roar
of the engine.

"Good plan!" replied Uncle Pete as he pulled back on the controls, added more power and soared higher and higher.

Up amongst the clouds they flew, then beyond their fluffy white tops to a place where the air was really cold and clear.

The sun was setting and the sky turned an amazing mixture of colours – dark blues, oranges and reds.

For a moment, Uncle Pete and TM forgot about the place they were trying to find, and just enjoyed the view from high above the Earth. They turned east, away from the setting sun, and flew on through the night in silence, thinking about how all the people in the world below them should come and take a look at the planet from up high and just forget all about arguing.

◆

The next morning was bright and sunny. Both TM and Uncle Pete had fallen asleep during the night, but the old plane had kept going in a straight line. TM rubbed her eyes as the sunlight warmed her whiskers and her tummy rumbled.

"What's for breakfast?" she asked Uncle Pete, who was awake and brushing his teeth.

"Hmm," he said. "The beans are finished and we're down to the last strawberry jam sandwich, I'm afraid. Let's cut it in half and make it last." TM's cheese was all finished too.

As they tucked into their halves of the very last strawberry jam sandwich, Uncle Pete started thinking about how they hadn't had to land for fuel since taking off. How long had they been flying? He couldn't remember. Maybe it was a week. Or perhaps a month. TM couldn't remember either. Uncle Pete was surprised by how good stardust was at powering the plane and how it was probably much better for the environment than the fuel he normally used.

Right then, the stardust ran out. The engine went silent, and the propeller stopped turning. The sparkly trail faded away and all that was left was the sound of the wind.

"Uh oh!" said TM.

"Uh oh, indeed," said Uncle Pete. "We probably need to land."

"Where?" said TM. "We're really high up above the clouds and I can't see any land, perhaps we should…"

But TM didn't get a chance to finish

what she was saying as the sky suddenly became very, very dark.

The Sun vanished and the Moon instantly popped into its place, like in a film that had been sped up. Seconds later, the sky became filled with more stars than TM could possibly have imagined even existed.

TM thought she was imaging the scene because she was pretty hungry by now. Or perhaps she was still asleep and this was a dream.

But it wasn't. Uncle Pete was shouting and pointing over the side of the plane. It was pitch dark though, so TM had no idea what he was pointing at. She climbed onto his shoulder for a better look.

Beneath the plane, through the inky darkness, there was a hole in the clouds. And through the hole TM could see a land shaped like a crescent moon, with high snowy mountains sparkling in blazing silver starlight.

"That's it! That's it!" yelled Uncle Pete waving the map. He pushed the silent old plane down towards the hole in the clouds and the strange land's mountains, which soared like enormous icy teeth into the night sky.

"There's still nowhere to land!" said TM. "It's all too jagged and snowy."

"That's why I have this!" replied Uncle Pete, pulling a very old and tatty looking parachute from behind his seat. "Stay in my pocket and hold on tight, TM, we're going in."

"Ok!" said TM, who never said no to a crazy adventure, even one that meant she had to jump out of a plane in the dark.

"What about the plane?" shouted TM.

"I expect it'll go and land somewhere safe and wait there until we can get to it," said Uncle Pete as he strapped the parachute on over his rucksack. "Or maybe it'll crash. I don't really know!"

"Well, ok," replied TM. "Let's do this!"

Uncle Pete glided the plane through the hole in the clouds and then, when he was almost directly above the jagged mountain range, he flipped the plane upside down.

"Now!" shouted Uncle Pete, letting go of the controls and dropping out of his seat. TM held on tightly to Uncle Pete's jacket pocket. The cold air rushed past her face as they fell faster and faster towards the fearsome looking mountains.

"Woooohoooo!" shouted TM in excitement. "This is amazing!"

"Hold on, TM!" shouted Uncle Pete. "I'm going to pull the release cord on the parachute. There'll be a big jolt, then we'll float down safely!"

"Ok!" replied TM, holding on to the inside of the pocket a little tighter.

"Three, two, one!" yelled Uncle Pete, then he pulled the cord on his parachute.

The top of the parachute bag opened

and, instead of a parachute, a load of Uncle Pete's underpants and dirty washing flew out into the sky.

"Ooops!" said Uncle Pete, watching all of his laundry stream out above their heads. "Wrong bag!"

"Oops?" shouted TM in alarm. "Ooops? Now what?"

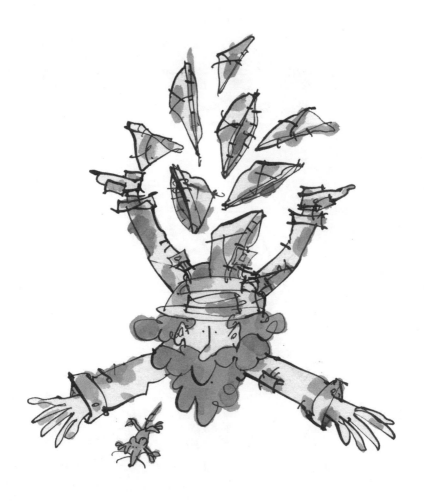

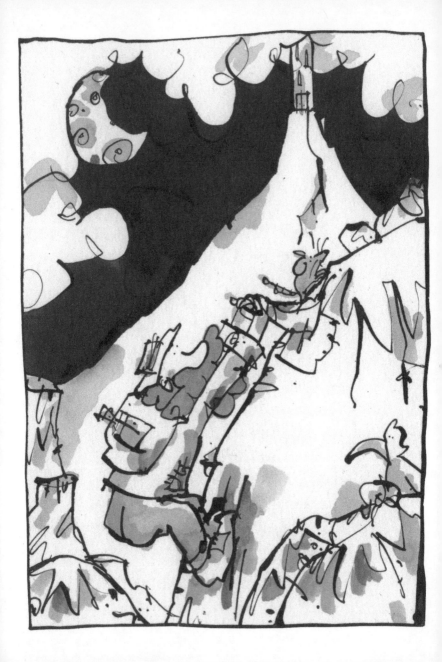

Chapter 5

Uncle Pete and TM fell faster and faster towards the icy mountains, watching the snow and rocks get closer and closer. TM was sure they were doomed, but she'd enjoyed the adventure and reckoned it had all been worth it.

Then the clouds closed in and they couldn't see the mountains below them anymore. TM was quite glad as she didn't really want to see them.

Uncle Pete was trying to figure out if he could make another parachute from the underpants he was wearing when they passed through a silvery cloud and slowed down slightly.

"Interesting," said Uncle Pete to himself.

They passed through another silvery cloud and slowed a little again.

"We're slowing down!" shouted TM. "The clouds are slowing us down."

Uncle Pete and TM stopped falling and, instead, were floating now through a thick blanket of moonlit cloud – it felt as if they were hardly moving.

They both cheered as they popped out of the bottom of the clouds and plopped softly and safely into deep snow on the side of the highest mountain. It stretched off for thousands of feet above them, with sides that looked impossible to climb.

Standing up, they brushed off the snow and gazed at the scene in front of them.

Uncle Pete, who was still holding onto the map, pointed at it, and then at the top of the mountain.

"Yep! This is the place, TM! We've found it. Come with me! We're going up there!"

"We're going up there?" asked TM, not really believing it.

"Yep," said Uncle Pete, showing her the

map. The place we need to get to is right at the very top of the mountain.

"Well, ok then," said TM. "Let's go."

They were both really hungry and very cold by now, but they began to climb up the steep sides of the mountain. TM was a great climber and she led the way up the icy rocks.

Uncle Pete had climbed loads of mountains as an explorer, so he was enjoying the experience and was impressed by how well TM could climb. They both got warm as they pushed on upwards in the moonlight.

After hours and hours, they arrived at the top of the mountain where, sparkling in the moonlight, stood a tall, silvery tower, its top hidden by the clouds.

"Made it!" shouted Uncle Pete, delighted.

"Do they have heating and cheese in there?" asked TM, pointing at the tower.

Uncle Pete and TM walked through the thick snow to the bottom of the tower and its big, black front door. There was a shiny square nameplate on the door, which read "Mr Nimbus T. Weaver. Please Knock Loudly". Uncle Pete knocked as hard as he could on the door using a knocker shaped just like a crescent moon.

After a while, Uncle Pete and TM heard footsteps from inside the tower. The door creaked open and there, standing in front of them, was a very tall, very old man. He had a thin, friendly face, with rosy cheeks, and a long silvery beard.

He wore a thick, black woolly jumper, covered in stars, which shimmered and winked in the moonlight. On top of his silvery hair was a black woolly hat, which also sparkled with tiny stars. Even his eyes twinkled like stars.

"Pete!" said the old man, shaking Uncle Pete's hand. "I haven't seen you for ages. What a wonderful surprise! And who's this?"

"I'm called TM," said TM, who was shivering with the cold by now. "PPPleased to meet you."

"Please come in, get warm and have some chips, beans on toast and strawberry jam," said Mr Weaver, beckoning them inside. "And I expect you'd like some cheese, TM!"

"Thank you," replied TM and Uncle Pete as they came inside Mr Weaver's tower. He had a huge fire burning in the fireplace in his round living room, but it was unlike any fire TM had seen before.

The flames weren't red and yellow – they were a shimmering silver. It looked cold and icy, but the fire was really warm and made the room very cosy.

After a huge tea of chips, beans, strawberry jam and cheese, Mr Weaver, Uncle Pete and TM all sat around the roaring silver fire on big comfy chairs. TM had loads of questions for Mr Weaver – why was it always dark in this place? Why did he live in this big tower? Why were there so many stars? But she politely said nothing as she knew they had important business to deal with.

"So, Pete. What brings you back here?" asked Mr Weaver.

Uncle Pete told him all about Harry

and how he'd never, ever slept. He told him about all the different things that Mum and Dad had tried to do to get him to sleep – the stories, the singing, the cows, the concerts – everything.

"He's never even had a dream!" added TM, who hadn't actually met Harry, but knew all about his story from Uncle Pete.

"Oh dear," said Mr Weaver, "that is a problem. But I'm happy to say that I can help. Please come with me."

Mr Weaver led Uncle Pete and TM up and up the winding stairs of his tower, which went on for ages. Just when Uncle Pete's legs were getting really tired, they reached the top where there were two big black wooden doors. Mr Weaver opened one of the doors and stepped outside onto a huge, fluffy cloud, lit by the light of the moon. It stretched off far into the distance.

"Welcome to my garden," he said.

There were no flowers in this cloud garden, only a single sheep. It was happily munching away at the cloud, which looked like silver candy floss in the moonlight. Its woolly coat was the deepest black, just like the old man's jumper, and it shimmered with the light from millions of tiny stars.

Mr Weaver walked across the cloud towards the sheep, bent down and whispered something in its ear. The sheep nodded and then went back to munching the cloud. Mr Weaver took a big pair of silver scissors from the pocket of his trousers and began clipping wool from the sheep's back. Uncle Pete and TM had to cover their eyes as bright stardust fell from the wool, while Mr Weaver snipped away at it.

When he had collected enough, Mr Weaver said thank you to the sheep, and carried the pile of soft, glittering wool back into the tower.

Once they were back inside, Mr Weaver opened the other door at the top of the stairs and led Uncle Pete and TM into another room. In a corner stood an old-fashioned spinning wheel and a big wooden loom that people used to make cloth on. There was also a washing machine, and an enormous black cat wearing glasses. It sat at a wooden desk, with a lamp, reading a book.

"Eeek!" screamed TM. "A cat!"

"Don't worry, TM," said Mr Weaver. "That's Inky. He's friendly."

"Meow," said Inky, who went back to reading his book.

Mr Weaver went over and spoke to Inky, who nodded and put his book down.

Inky then took the pile of sparking black
wool from Mr Weaver and placed it in the
washing machine.

Standing on a chair, Inky reached
up and took a jam jar full of twinkling

coloured lights down from a shelf.

"Stand back," Mr Weaver said to Uncle Pete and TM as Inky unscrewed the lid of the jar and poured it into the top of the washing machine.

"What kind of washing up powder is that?" asked TM, her eyes wide in amazement.

"Those are dreams," said Mr Weaver.

"I think I must be dreaming," said TM, shaking her head. "I've never seen anything like that."

"You're a talking mouse," laughed Mr Weaver. "Anything is possible. Now, watch this."

Inky closed the washing machine door and turned it on. Uncle Pete and TM watched as the machine began to slowly churn, and then spin faster and faster.

They could see the wool inside, going around and around, mixing with the dazzling dream lights. It became a blur of starlight and colours they'd never seen before, and then stopped. The washing machine beeped.

"Meow," said Inky as he opened the washing machine door and took out the sparkling black wool. He held it over the empty jar and squeezed, and the coloured lights poured out of the wool, like a rainbow coming out of a tap.

Inky screwed the lid back on and placed the lights back on the shelf.

He then carried the wool to the

spinning wheel, sat down and began to spin it into yarn – a kind of thick thread used to knit. His paws were a blur and, seconds later, Inky had a big spindle of sparkly black woollen yarn.

"Meow," said Inky, nodding his head.

"I agree," said Mr Weaver. Inky attached the spindle of woollen yarn to the loom and off he went again, paws moving faster than lightning, the loom clattering away, noisily.

"What's he making?" asked TM.

"Wait and see," said Mr Weaver. "Just wait and see."

A few minutes later, the loom stopped and Inky sat back in his chair. "Meow," he said, satisfied.

Mr Weaver walked over to the loom and lifted from it the most amazing woollen blanket Uncle Pete and TM had ever seen. It was like looking at the blackest and starriest of night skies. Amongst the billions of stars twinkling and glittering on its deep black cloth, were lots of crescent moons, shining like diamonds.

"This should be just the thing," said Mr Weaver. "Wrap young Harry in this, and he'll have the best night's sleep and the finest of dreams."

"Fantastic!" said Uncle Pete. "It's beautiful! Thank you so much! And thank you too, Inky. What can we give you both in return for your kindness?"

"Nothing!" said Mr Weaver, smiling.

"It's a gift from Inky and me and the best thing in the world is being kind to people. You're my friend and we're helping you, and that brings me the greatest of pleasure."

"Thank you, Mr Weaver." said TM, her eyes filling up with tiny tears. "Thank you, Inky."

"Meow."

"We don't want to be rude, Mr Weaver, but we'll have to leave right away to get this beautiful blanket back to Harry," said Uncle Pete.

But then Uncle Pete remembered something pretty important. "Oh, no! we jumped out of our plane to get here and it will take years to walk home," he said, slapping himself on the head. "We'll never get the blanket to Harry for ages now!"

Chapter 6

"Ah, don't you worry, Pete," said Mr Weaver, his thin face beaming in a smile. "Follow me."

Inky went back to reading his book. Uncle Pete rolled up the shimmering blanket and placed it carefully into his rucksack as the old man led him and TM back out onto the cloud. The sheep was still there, munching away.

They all walked past the sheep this time and out towards the edge of the cloud where a flight of fluffy steps dropped down into the darkness. Uncle Pete and TM couldn't see where the steps led to, but they followed Mr Weaver, down and down.

Eventually, the steps stopped. Uncle Pete and TM felt as if they were standing on the edge of a huge drop, but there was something floating nearby in the darkness.

"Maybe you'd like to borrow this to get home?" asked Mr Weaver, throwing a pocketful of stardust into the air. It lit up a cloud that was shaped like a ship. The ship had a mast of ice and a black sail that shimmered and sparkled, just like the woollen blanket. A silvery anchor attached to a rope held the ship in place at the bottom of the cloud steps.

"Wow! A cloud ship?" asked TM. "How does it float? Are we next to the sea?"

Mr Weaver chuckled. "It's for sailing the Night Ocean, TM."

"How fast can it go?

"You'll just have to try it and see, TM," laughed Mr Weaver.

"Amazing! Thank you, Mr Weaver," said Uncle Pete. "But how do we get it back to you?"

"Set it free when you reach home," replied Mr Weaver. "It'll find its way back to me, don't worry. Oh, and look inside the wooden box on the deck. There's something in there for you both."

"Thank you for your kindness, Mr Weaver," said Uncle Pete, giving Mr Weaver a hug. "We'll come back to visit sometime."

"You are always welcome, Pete," said Mr Weaver. "You too, TM. Remember, anything is possible."

Uncle Pete and TM carefully stepped into the cloud ship. It rocked gently. TM looked over the side but could see only deep darkness.

Mr Weaver lifted the silvery anchor and threw it off the edge of the cloud steps. Uncle Pete pulled it in by its rope and placed it on the deck. Mr Weaver then

gave the ship a gentle push. It drifted away
from the cloud steps, its black shimmering
sail filling with moonlight.

"Hold on tight!" shouted Mr Weaver, as
the ship pulled away from the cloud steps.
Uncle Pete and TM waved goodbye, but

the ship was already moving fast through the darkness, its sail brightly lit. They looked back towards the mountain and Mr Weaver's tower, but they were gone.

"There's the box!" said TM, pointing towards the big wooden box that was sitting in the middle of the deck. It was decorated with silver stars and moons.

Uncle Pete opened it and inside were two sparkly black woolly jumpers, just like Mr Weaver's. One was the right size for Uncle Pete, the other a tiny one for TM. There were loads and loads of strawberry jam sandwiches, several tins of beans and two enormous lumps of cheese.

And beside the jumpers and all the food, were six jam jars full of stardust, just like the stuff Uncle Pete had used in his plane's fuel tank. There was a note from Mr Weaver stuck to one of the jars. It said: "To Pete and TM. I thought you might find this stardust useful in your adventures. Inky knitted the jumpers and hopes you'll like them. Safe travels, love Mr Weaver and Inky."

There was a paw print next to his signature which they guessed was Inky's, and the word "Meow".

The cloud ship sailed through the sky at incredible speed, way faster than Uncle Pete's plane had travelled. Uncle Pete and TM, both wearing their woolly jumpers, held tightly onto its big wheel and tried to steer, but then started to feel as if the ship knew where it had to take them. After a while, they relaxed and began to eat their sandwiches and beans, watching the sail above their heads filled with moonlight.

TM wondered what would happen when the daylight came and the moon went away. But the moon stayed out, its light continuing to push the sail of the cloud ship. For days they sailed fast through the darkness, with the moon behind them, driving them onwards.

TM pointed to a shooting star, soaring across the dark sky. The ship was keeping up with it, they were travelling so fast.

"Look!" said Uncle Pete, pointing over the side of the ship. "Whales!"

"Whales?" said TM, who thought Uncle Pete was joking. "There can't be any whales up here!"

But there were. These looked a bit different from the whales in the ocean back down on Earth though. They were the same shape – huge and sleek, with enormous gentle eyes – but they glowed silver in the moonlight. They were fast too, swimming effortlessly through the night ocean beneath the cloud ship, singing and talking to one another in the way whales do. It was an eerie and beautiful sound.

And there were dolphins – also glowing silver in the moonlight. They played near the bow of the ship as it cut through the black of the sky. It was an awesome sight.

Now and again, TM was sure she could see other cloud ships travelling through the darkness with moonlight filled sails, but she also thought she might be dreaming. This adventure had been so incredible, and she had seen so many wonderful things that just didn't seem possible.

She thought about her family and how amazed they'd be to see what she was doing now. It made her sad to think about them, and tiny tears filled her eyes. Uncle Pete noticed she was looking a bit sad and knew just what was wrong.

"Don't worry, TM. Your family loved you and they'd be very proud to see how brave you are now. And you're not alone anymore."

"Thank you, Uncle Pete," said TM, drying her eyes.

Uncle Pete and TM looked out over the side of the ship, watching the stars, the whales and the dolphins pass by, listening to their songs. They were warm in their sparkly woollen jumpers and looking forward to getting their amazing gift back to Harry.

"How far do you think we have to go?" asked TM.

"I've no idea," replied Uncle Pete. "We're going so fast though; I can't imagine it will be much longer until we get home."

Chapter 7

Uncle Pete and TM were just about to share some cheese and strawberry jam sandwiches – TM had invented those, and they were great – when the ship began to slow down.

"Perhaps we're nearly home!" said TM, excitedly.

"Hmm, I'm not so sure," replied Uncle Pete. "Look."

The stars had all disappeared. The whales and dolphins were no longer travelling by their side either. The moon vanished behind some very menacing dark clouds and the ship stopped. It began to rock from side to side and they felt as if they were on a rough sea, but there were no waves to be seen, just deep, dark blackness. There was no sound either. No howling wind, no rain or hailstones. Only silence.

"It must be some kind of weird storm!" shouted Uncle Pete as the ship dipped down and then up again. The ship's wheel spun around, out of control. "We need to try and steer through it!"

Without the moonlight, the ship was

adrift and at the mercy of the storm. As an explorer, Uncle Pete had survived many storms at sea, but this one was different. They were in a ship made of clouds, thousands of feet up, in the pitch dark.

The ship rolled and rocked and spun around. TM and Uncle Pete held onto the wheel, trying to keep the ship going in a straight line. They were far too busy to feel seasick.

Uncle Pete and TM were both wondering if the ship would just fall apart – it was made of clouds, after all – sending them falling back to earth, but they didn't share their fears and kept holding onto the steering wheel.

They could see nothing but felt as if they

were riding the biggest waves imaginable. Up and down they went, hoping to see a star or the moon again, but all around them was emptiness.

The silent storm raged for what felt like years to Uncle Pete and TM. They spun around in the darkness, clinging to the wheel, with no idea of where they were or where they were heading – forwards, backwards, upside down – they just didn't know.

The ship began to rear up, like it was being drawn up the face of a giant wave, one they couldn't see.

"Hold the wheel, TM!" shouted Uncle Pete as he reached for the wooden box – he'd sensibly tied it down with some rope – and pulled out a jar of stardust. He unscrewed the lid, scooped out a handful of the dust and then threw it into the air above the ship.

For the briefest of moments, the stardust illuminated the ship and everything around it. Uncle Pete wished he couldn't see again as, just like he'd feared, the ship was being pulled up the face of the biggest, darkest, heaviest, most terrifying wave he'd ever seen. It was black, silent and beginning to fall over at the top. He was sure it would capsize the ship, turning it upside down and sending them tumbling into the night.

But just as the light from the stardust faded, there was a loud thump beneath the ship. And then another, and another. The ship stopped rolling and rocking quite so much. Another loud thump and it straightened up. A fifth thump and they felt as if they were travelling up the front of the giant wave much faster. Perhaps they'd make it, though Uncle Pete had no idea what was happening.

"What was that?" shouted TM. "Have we hit something?"

"No!" shouted Uncle Pete, looking over the side of the ship. "It's the whales! They're back and they're carrying the ship!"

Sure enough, the ship was surrounded by the silvery glowing whales. They'd pressed their huge bodies against either

side of the ship to stop it from rocking. Several whales were pushing it from behind, driving it onwards to the top of the enormous dark wave.

"Thank you!" yelled Uncle Pete and TM to the whales. They didn't reply as they were concentrating so hard on their task.

Uncle Pete and TM felt the ship reach the top of the giant wave and then plummet down the other side, but the whales kept them steady, guiding them through the storm.

On and on they pushed through more giant dark and angry waves until the air became smooth once again and the moon and stars reappeared. The sails filled with moonlight, the whales turned away from the ship, and it began to move on its own once again.

Uncle Pete and TM watched as the whales lifted their enormous fins, as if waving goodbye, and then they were gone, swallowed up in the darkness.

It was a smooth journey from then on,

though Uncle Pete and TM kept a careful watch for ominous black clouds.

Further on in their voyage, they ran into a shower of small shooting stars, which made lots of little holes in the sail. TM climbed up the mast and repaired the shimmering cloth with patches made from a pair of Uncle Pete's spare (and clean) underpants. They worked just fine.

A day or so later, they noticed they were being followed by a gigantic silvery shark. The ship sped up, and so did the shark. Uncle Pete and TM could see its big black eyes watching them. It swam under the ship and gave it a nudge with its nose, investigating. Uncle Pete and TM felt the bump – it was a very big shark.

"We're just on our way home!" Uncle Pete shouted over the side of the ship. "We don't want any bother. Would you like a sandwich? We have strawberry jam and cheese!"

The shark made a disgusted face and swam off.

Later, Uncle Pete was surprised to see his old plane off in the distance, high above them, the moonlight illuminating its red wings. It looked as if it was being carried along by the night ocean currents, but in a totally different direction to the one the cloud ship was travelling.

"Well I never," he said. "We must remember to go and find that after we get home, TM."

They watched as the plane became a tiny speck and then vanished in the dark.

"Home," said TM, sadly. "I don't have a home anymore. I was sleeping in your plane, remember? It's gone now, so I guess I'll have to move on and find somewhere else to live."

"What?" said Uncle Pete. "Nonsense! We're family now, a team! Your home is with me and you can come on all my adventures. If you'd like, of course!"

"Yes! Thank you!" said TM. "I'd love to!"

"That's it settled then."

"Are all your adventures as crazy and magical as this one?" asked TM.

"Well, there was this one time…"

But Uncle Pete didn't get a chance to finish his story as, right at that moment, the ship stopped.

"Storm? Shark? Shooting Stars?" asked TM.

"Nope," said Uncle Pete. "It looks as if we're back."

Chapter 8

Uncle Pete looked over the side of the ship, which was rocking gently about 20 feet just above the garden behind Harry's house.

It was nighttime in the town and the streets were silent. Of course, the lights were on in Harry's house as he was still awake.

"Well, there you go!" said Uncle Pete, throwing the ship's icy anchor over the side. The rope it was attached to zipped off into the darkness. There was a loud crash as the anchor fell through the shed in Harry's garden, destroying it. Dogs started barking and more lights in the street came on.

"Oops," said Uncle Pete. "Never mind!"

Uncle Pete tied another rope to the wooden box with the jars of stardust and empty bean tins – he always took his rubbish home – and lowered it to the ground. Then he and TM threw a rope ladder over the side of the ship and began to climb down into the garden.

Once they were on the ground, Uncle

Pete took out his enormous explorer knife and cut the anchor rope. The cloud ship floated up slightly, turned and then sailed off back the way it had come, whatever way that was.

"Thank you!" shouted Uncle Pete and TM, but the ship was gone in the blink of an eye.

Uncle Pete hammered on the front door of Harry's house, but Dad was already coming out to see what the loud crash was from the garden.

"What are you doing back so soon?" he asked Uncle Pete when he saw him on the doorstep. "I thought you said you were going to meet someone who could help Harry. You've only been gone a few minutes. And why is there a mouse in your pocket?"

"Good evening!" said TM to Dad.

"The mouse talks? The mouse talks!" Dad was astonished.

"Yes, I can talk," said TM, rolling her eyes as Uncle Pete ran past Dad without even saying hello. He went into the living room where Harry was still sorting out all of his school things for the next day. Mum was fast asleep on the sofa.

"Uncle Pete!" said Harry. "How come you're back so quickly? And why's there a mouse in your pocket?"

"Hello, Harry," said TM. "Pleased to meet you. I'm TM."

"Um, hello TM, pleased to meet you too," replied Harry.

He was just about to ask Uncle Pete about the polite talking mouse he'd brought along, when Uncle Pete said: "Put your jammies on and get into bed, quickly!"

Harry shrugged, ran upstairs, changed into his jammies and got tucked up in bed, confused about what was happening, but excited to meet a talking mouse.

Uncle Pete and TM came upstairs and into the bedroom, followed by Dad and Mum, who had woken up. She rubbed her eyes and was just about to ask Uncle Pete why there was a mouse sitting on the end of Harry's bed, when Uncle Pete pulled the blanket he'd got from Mr Weaver out of his rucksack.

The blanket shimmered, filling the bedroom with soft starlight. It even made the room feel lovely and warm.

"Wow!" said Harry. "What's THAT?"

Mum and Dad's eyes were wide. "It's

as if someone has unrolled the night sky," said Mum. "I've never seen anything like it!"

"Wrap it around you, Harry!" said TM. Harry wasn't going to argue with a talking mouse, so he wrapped the twinkling blanket around himself. He had never felt anything so soft, warm and cosy.

And then Harry started to feel something new. He felt…he wasn't sure what it was. Could it be…sleepy? His eyes got heavier and heavier and then he did something else he'd never done before. He yawned. It felt good. His head gently fell onto his pillow, his eyes closed, and Harry fell sound asleep for the very first time in his life.

"Mission accomplished," whispered Uncle Pete to TM, who gave him a thumbs up.

"Yessss!" said Mum and Dad, quietly, before bursting into happy tears. They hugged Uncle Pete and TM and thanked them for their wonderful gift.

Leaving Harry snoring away under the magical blanket, they all went downstairs for some supper. Mum and Dad wanted to ask Uncle Pete and TM lots of questions about the blanket and their adventure. They could hardly believe Uncle Pete and TM when they said they'd been travelling for weeks, maybe even longer. But before they could eat and find out more about their journey and all the amazing things they'd seen, Mum and Dad fell asleep with their heads on the table.

"Let's go and cook up some beans on toast back home," said Uncle Pete to TM.

"Will there be cheese?" asked TM.

"Definitely, TM. There will always be cheese from now on."

Uncle Pete closed his rucksack and put it on his back. TM scurried up into Uncle Pete's pocket. Uncle Pete then wrote a note to Mum, Dad and Harry saying TM and he were off home for some food. He said they'd be leaving again soon on another adventure, probably to try and find the plane, and that it might be a few years before they saw them again.

Switching off all the lights in the house, Uncle Pete and TM walked out of the door, closing it quietly behind them. They collected the box full of stardust jars and empty bean tins and began the long walk back to the forest and Uncle Pete's home, talking about their adventure.

That night Harry had a sleep that

made up for all the sleeps he had missed in his life. And he also had his very first dream, where he flew across the night in a plane powered only by stardust, exploring distant lands that nobody else had ever seen.

And did Uncle Pete and TM ever find the plane? Well, you'll just have to wait and see.

The end

DAVID C. FLANAGAN is a writer and award-winning journalist based in the Orkney Islands. Born, raised and educated in Edinburgh, he studied journalism in the city before returning to his ancestral home in the islands where he worked as a reporter on the local weekly newspaper, *The Orcadian*. He's been freelance since 2002, providing news, features and content for a variety of publications and websites. David also acts as location manager for film and television crews operating in Orkney.

His first book, *Board*, was published by Fledgling Press in 2015 and recounted his hapless attempts to learn to surf in middle age, on the wild Atlantic coast of Orkney. He still surfs, badly, and also loves skateboarding, fitness training and walking in the Scottish mountains.

Uncle Pete and the Boy Who Couldn't Sleep is David's first story for children, reflecting his passion for adventure stories, his love of animals, and his slightly whacky sense of humour.

WILL HUGHES is a young illustrator and cartoonist, recently graduated from Edinburgh College of Art. Whatever he makes, whether it is stories, cartoons or prints, he likes his work to be comic and humorous, and to tell the stories of all sorts of ridiculous things. From a old woman with a hoard of very helpful cats to burglars who have to stand on each others shoulders to rob a house. He usually draws these with a dipping ink pen and watercolour paints to create energetic, lively and fluid lines and colours. Will's debut picture book *What Not To Give An Ogre For His Birthday* was published by Little Door Books in 2019 and is available to order online and from all good bookshops.

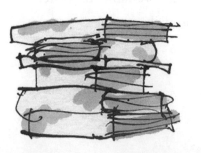

Turn over for a
sneak peek of
Uncle Pete's
next adventure

...

Uncle Pete
and the
Forest of Lost Things

Chapter 1

"I'm not scared of you!" shouted TM at the enormous cats surrounding her. But inside, she was feeling really scared and the cats knew it. They could see her trembling slightly as she stood looking up at them, even though she was trying to look brave.

These were pretty scary cats though, even if you normally like cats. If you can imagine an elephant wearing a cat costume to a Halloween party, then that's how big these cats were. You'd definitely not want one of them curled up on your knee, or scratching your sofa.

And they certainly weren't in the mood for any kind of party now they'd been disturbed by a tiny, shouty mouse.

There were 12 of them, all different colours – ginger, white and ginger, black and white, black, grey and beige. There were some tabby ones with stripes too. The cats had formed a circle around TM and sat, tails flicking, looking down at her, waiting to see what she would do next.

TM hadn't noticed the cats at first because she was so exhausted, hungry and thirsty. She'd been walking through this endless forest for weeks and weeks, with no idea of what direction she was travelling.

When TM had finally emerged from the trees into a clearing in the forest, she was almost asleep and shuffling along with her head down, not seeing the cats sunning themselves on some flat rocks.

She'd woken up pretty quickly when she bumped into a huge cat paw, with giant claws poking through thick ginger fur. Her eyes suddenly wide and her heart hammering away, TM had tried to sneak backwards into the forest, but the cats had spotted her as she trudged out of the trees and quietly surrounded her.

TM was now trying very hard not to make any sudden moves. She was also determined not to think about the sad and scary time she'd lost all of her family to a normal sized cat.

She'd managed to escape back then and had ended up finding a new home with Uncle Pete.

She thought of the amazing adventure they'd shared too, flying to a strange night-time land in Uncle Pete's old plane, eating beans on toast, strawberry jam sandwiches and lots of cheese. They'd met Mr Weaver and a sheep with sparkling starlight wool, and then travelled home in a cloud ship with a special blanket to help Uncle Pete's nephew Harry finally get to sleep.

TM had been so happy during the adventure and felt as if she'd found a new family too, with Uncle Pete and all the animals that lived around his home in the forest. It was a nice forest. Not like this one with the giant cats.

Weeks and weeks ago, TM and Uncle Pete had set off on another adventure. They'd gone looking for Uncle Pete's plane which had flown away by itself into the Night Ocean after they'd jumped out of it and landed on Mr Weaver's icy mountain.

TM and Uncle Pete had been really excited about their new adventure together, packing lots and lots of beans, cheese and strawberry jam before setting out. TM had pulled her big, heavy rucksack onto her back, and said: "Let's go!"

But now she was on her own again,

surrounded by giant cats in a forest with no end…

One of the giant cats started cleaning its bum, just like your pet cat does, but another – the biggest of them all – hissed "Tiddles! This is not the time for that! We have…a guest."

Tiddles looked embarrassed, stopped cleaning himself and tried to look fierce again.

"You can talk?" shouted TM to the biggest cat – a huge white and ginger one which she thought must be the leader.

"Of course I can talk," growled the cat. "We all can. We're The Cats of The Forest of Lost Things. But we've never seen a talking mouse before."

"You're all lost too?" replied TM, suddenly wondering if she had something in common with these giant moggies.

"Yes," growled the cat. "Each of our owners thought we were too fussy as we kept changing our minds about the kind of food we liked. Can you BELIEVE that?"

TM shook her head.

"Anyway, our owners threw us out and, in time, we all found our way to this forest," the cat continued. "It's really big and it's impossible to get out of here, as you've discovered, so it's our home now. We had to eat most of the small animals and birds that lived here, and then moved on to eating bigger things, which is why we've all grown so much."

The cat leaned forward and put his massive pink nose right in TM's face. His incredibly long whiskers twitched a little and then he asked: "Are you alone, mouse?"

TM gulped, but tried not to look worried. Would she be the next snack on the forest menu for these enormous moggies? Would she ever see Uncle Pete again?...

To be continued...